Nuclear Weapons Are Now Illegal – "Our Way Forward"

Poems and Reflections

by Al Drinkwine

Dedication

We learn from each of our children as they teach us an abundance of truths. Profoundly grateful for the lessons our three children have taught me, I dedicate this to our three beautiful children and extended families with there children.

Foreword

With all our recent political, social, medical, and spiritual concerns, the most threatening need on our planet appears to have been closeted far too long. I honestly believe history, when forgotten, or ignored, can repeat itself. The following nuclear facts indicate this may be true.

Hiroshima and Nagasaki, Japan--August 1945--United States atomic bombs militarily dropped on both cities. An estimated 110,00 individuals died, and an estimated 130,000 individuals were injured or wounded.

Windscale--Cumberland (now Cumbria), UK--October 1957--More than 200 cancer deaths resulted.

Sodium Reactor Experiment--Los Angeles, California July 1959.

SL-1--Idaho Falls, Idaho--January 1961--Three workers received lethal doses of radiation.

Enrico Fermi Unit 1--Monroe County, Michigan--October 1966.

Three Mile Island--Middletown, Pennsylvania--March 1978.

Chernobyl, Ukraine (former Soviet Union)--April 1986--An estimated 125,000 individuals died, and thousands were relocated. Over three decades later, Chernobyl remains a ghost town.

Fukushima, Japan--March 2011--An earthquake and tsunami cut power to reactors causing a chain reaction forcing the evacuation of over 154,00 people. A "difficult to return" zone remains evacuated.

Our redirection of excessive nuclear and military funds to human services will benefit our entire world. Wouldn't it be beautiful to see the

COVID and future pandemics manageable? To have proper mental health treatment will improve millions of lives while reducing dangerous or addictive self-medications and homelessness. Redirected excessive spending can facilitate improved world health. A change of attitudes can make this a reality.

As a society, we have allowed governments and military related establishments to hold us hostage far too long. It is time to make our social concerns visible to those we select to support our needs and concerns. Change depends upon us. Each of us.

Contents

Chapter One
Hope Inspires

Please God

Dear God,
Father of all creation,
Please help us establish universal peace
on Your earthly plantation,
without further
procrastination ~

Our Focus

Sometimes, as we travel life's paths
our forest becomes troubled
with doubt, pain, fear, and anxiety

No weapons
can effectively shoot holes
in life's clouds of despair

However,
as we raise our eyes
glimpses of sunlight
filters through life's canopy of leaves
nourishing all life
tucked in the forest shadows

Hope,
enlightens our path

A smile
A cookie
A gentle wave

Can send problems
to their deserving grave

Let our focus
not hide in life's shadows

Allowing it to rise
to sunlit skies ~

~

Reflection One
Opening Our Minds
and Hearts

A suggestion for reading the following is to quietly reflect on each message as the intent of this book is to shed light on our varied paths for our human survival. Hopefully, with adequate light, shadowed realities will become visible.

As we have experienced, pandemics are merciless. But science, together with superb medical care family and friends, and individual faith and hope, healing can take place. Life can be amazing when we work together for our common cause. This is why the nuclear topic must be resurfaced, discussed, and addressed. Not all situations are reversable. So, the time has arrived to shine light on international shadows now camouflaged as our radiant security blanket. Our survival as one human family, living on one shared planet, depends on each of us.

Life survives under the premise we are each called to "love one another." The questions we seriously need to discuss openly and jointly are--do nuclear weapons represent this love? Do nuclear weapons deliver love? Is a nuclear war survivable?

As a society, we have closeted these issues far too long.

At present, there is an international threat. If nuclear weapons accidentally or intentionally be released, there is NO way out. This threat is far beyond healing through scientific, medical, or faith. This threat has the capability to eradicate life as we know it. This threat is scientifically designed, developed, constructed, and set for instant release. All life is at the disposal of instantaneous, stress filled human decisions and discretion.

We all know quite well how short tempered some decisionmakers can be. As an example, I will share an experience I had while employed with the

US Navy, at our nation's largest nuclear installation. Facilities at then, Naval Submarine Base Bangor, were being developed for the arrival of our first Trident nuclear submarine. While monitoring the installation of the telephone system, for the underground Trident Command Center one experience remains unforgettable. The telephone installation was nearing completion. Remaining was a final system-wide phone check which would be made that night after midnight pacific standard time. The entire facility staff was made aware of this critical test and advised not to use the phone system after midnight, prior to system clearance. This awareness included the commanding officer in charge of the Pacific Nuclear Fleet.

When I arrived early the next morning, I was informed by the installation supervisor that the test would need to be rescheduled due to a mishap. He explained the commanding officer had returned to work after midnight and attempted to make a phone call to Pearl Harbor, Hawaii. When he heard a voice interrupt his call, reminding him of the test, the commander slammed his receiver down so hard he smashed his office phone.

Is this the mentality we need in control of our nuclear-weaponed submarines?

Please, take the following into deep consideration. Our shared world depends on your understanding and assistance. We are in this together.

Hope Inspired

As life's path twists and turns,
For health, hope, and healing,
Our existence yearns

As fresh starts repeat
Life becomes sweet
With forward movement
Life keeps its beat

Ups and downs,
Joy and frowns,
Round-abouts,
Some dancing with clowns

Celebrations,
Joy and strife,
Blended grief,
Flows with life

The bridges we cross,
The mountains we climb,
Determine the memories
Left behind

Life's not a process
Through which we impress
We simply desire
To do our best

Asking our Creator
To assist
With the rest ~

~

Whispered Prayer

Anger
Starts wars

Anger
Closes doors

So what,
Is anger for

A rotting stump
With roots so deep

As through our heart
Those roots do creep

But deep within
Our human heart

Composted anger
Nourishes the heart

Providing hope
A fresh spring start ~

~

Heavenly Humanity

Discrimination
Of any form
Is the curse of division
Reborn and reborn

It is not from God
Nor born with His Son
It is direct form man
Discrimination, is human spun

For our God of love
Created us each
In His image
To cherish, love, and teach

Our God of love
Gifted humankind
With unconditional unity
Nowhere else can we find

So, as we unwrap
Our gifts of love
May we each and all
Give thanks to above ~

~

Decisions

Amazing matter
Sits between our ears
Sorting and sifting
What it sees, feels, and hears

This seldom seen matter
Prefers words that flatter
Separating concerns
From frivolous chatter

Our invisible mind
Helps us outline
Giving our thoughts and actions
A physical spine

Are our colorless thoughts
Exclusive or inclusive
Are our actions
Gentle or abusive

Do we squish the bug
And kick it under a rug
Or dubious thoughts
Prefer to unplug

Wouldn't it be nice
If life was that easy
But some thoughts
Are slippery and sleazy

That's where decisions
Come into play
It is our decision
What we do and say

What enters our mind
Need not control our actions
We can sort and sift
Discarding distractions
Discrimination
Does exist
Do we open our arms
Or close our fist ~

~

E pluribus Unum

In preferring to be constructive
We cannot ignore our destructive
For a damaged foundation
Can destroy our nation

When life's infection
Invades our head
We cannot close our eyes
And stay in bed

Indifference allows
The infection to spread
When pain and death
Continues to be feed

Our wisest move
Is to address the pain
With nothing to lose
We have national health to gain

We the people
Our nation of one
Has so much healing
That needs to be done

To do so the source
Of our infection must be treated
Replaced with healing
And fresh ground reseeded

To restore
Our nation's foundation
We must address multiple forms
Of infective discrimination

Equality
Provides a fresh start
As it flows from our head
Circulated by each heart

To circulate
Through each body part
Each and every one
Is called to take part

As we replace weapons
With a nonviolent vaccine
E pluribus Unum
Joyfully blooms on our scene

For the repair
To our national well-being
In God We Trust
Is the source of our vaccine

When spiritually injected
Hope is detected ~

~

Hope Blooms Abundantly

As we pray for safety
And unity
Let us do so unitedly
And confidently

For the God of creation
In whom we trust
Has infused hope
With a forward thrust

For as spring moves forth
Blooming around our nation
God has sent despair
On an extended vacation

So as despair
Sunbathes in hell
Prosperity will bloom
For an extended spell ~

Chapter Two
Closeted Reality

" Integrity is doing the right thing
even when no one is watching"

C. S. Lewis

Reflection Two
Our Review Mirror

The reality of the destructive potential of nuclear weapons, killing thousands of innocent civilians combined with the threat they currently dominate human life with, played a heavy role in my decision to resign my position with our nuclear navy. The excessive wasteful abuse of our tax dollars, which I have repeatedly witnessed, added to my desire to seek alternative employment. The following pictures add evidence to my decision. It is my sincere hope scenes like this will never be repeated anywhere on earth. To prevent this, we all need to become actively involved in nuclear disarmament. As the following pictures illustrate, nuclear weapons cannot be ignored.

As a result of our COVID 19 pandemic, our medical facilities became stressed for supplies, additional staffing, and hospital beds. Families need income to pay rent and buy food. An increase in homeless individuals and families, restaurants and business have closed. Schools need funding, along with numerous other essential needs. According to a CNN report the US spent $35.4 billion in 2019 on approximately 5,800* nuclear weapons. How far could $35.4 billion have gone to provide for life saving essentials, rather than weapons of mass destruction? Are our choices based on actual need, or fallacies that mislead?

> *Note: the actual number of nuclear weapons we have varies according to the source of information. Due to the classified facts, it is difficult to obtain an actual count. Sometimes I wonder if our government even knows the actual count.

The following historic pictures were selected from a variety of internet sources with Getty Images as the main source. Not wanting to distract attention from the images, many have no narrative. They speak for themselves.

Shattered Pearls

December 7th, 1941
Japan shattered American pearls
triggering revenge.

For nearly four years
the United States studied
and planed for their revenge
of our shattered pearls.

On August 6th and 9th, 1945
our revenge killed
between 129,000 and 226,000
civilians

Shattering Japan's pearls.

How lovable
are shattered pearls ~

The following images make visible the results of revenge.

Nagasaki

Enola Gay, the B-29 bomber that was used by the United States on August 6, 1945, to drop an atomic bomb on Hiroshima, Japan, the first time the explosive device had been used on an enemy target. The aircraft was named after the mother of pilot Paul Warfield Tibbets, Jr

About 44% of the city was destroyed; 35,000 people were killed and 60,000 injured.

On **9 August 1945**, Bockscar, piloted by the 393rd Bombardment Squadron's commander, Major Charles W. Sweeney, dropped the "Fat Man" nuclear bomb with a blast yield equivalent to 21 kilotons of TNT over the city of Nagasaki.

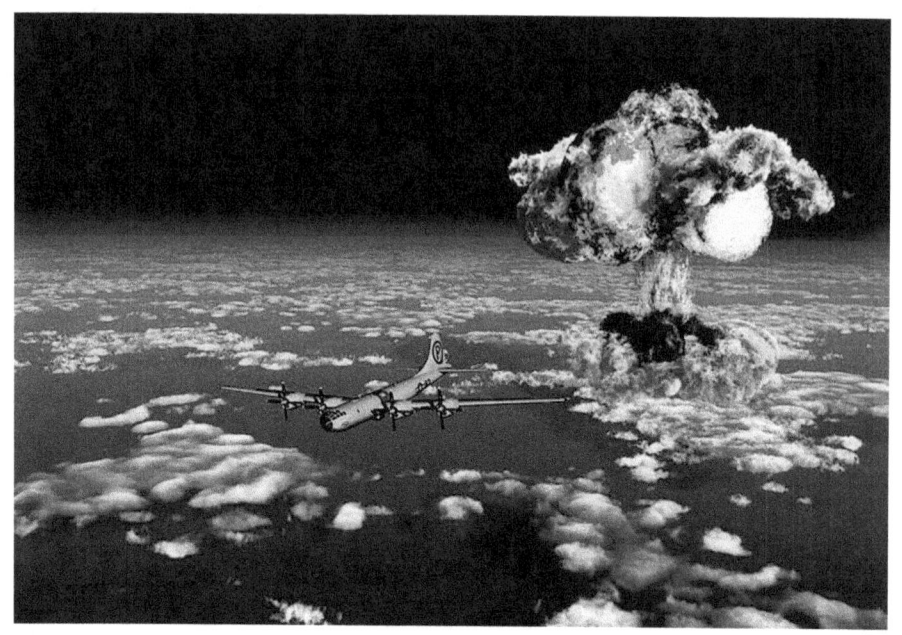

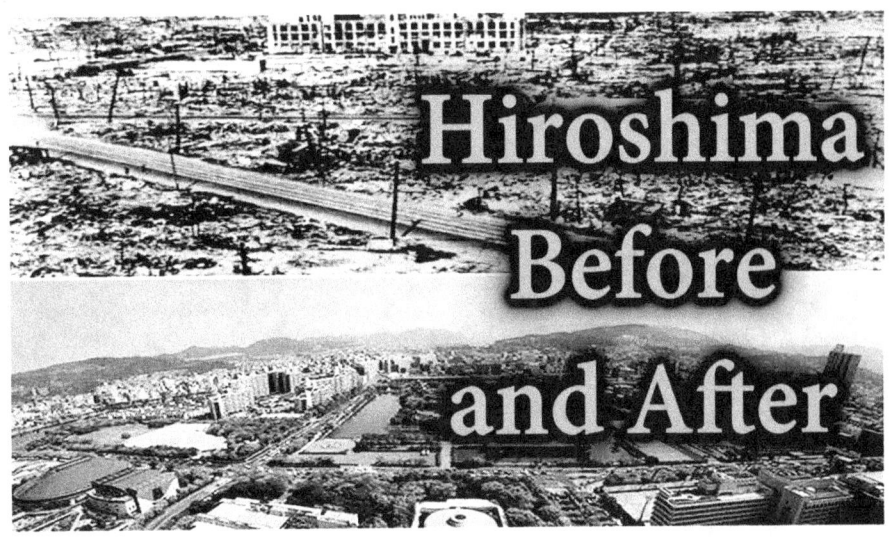

Atomic cloud over Nagasaki, 09.08.1945 Photo by Hiromihi Matsuda

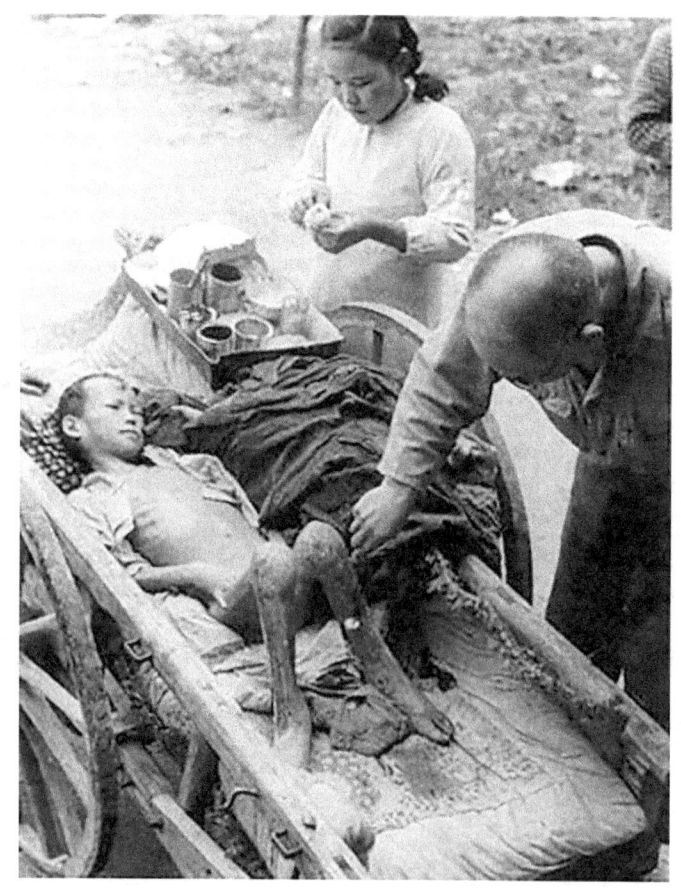

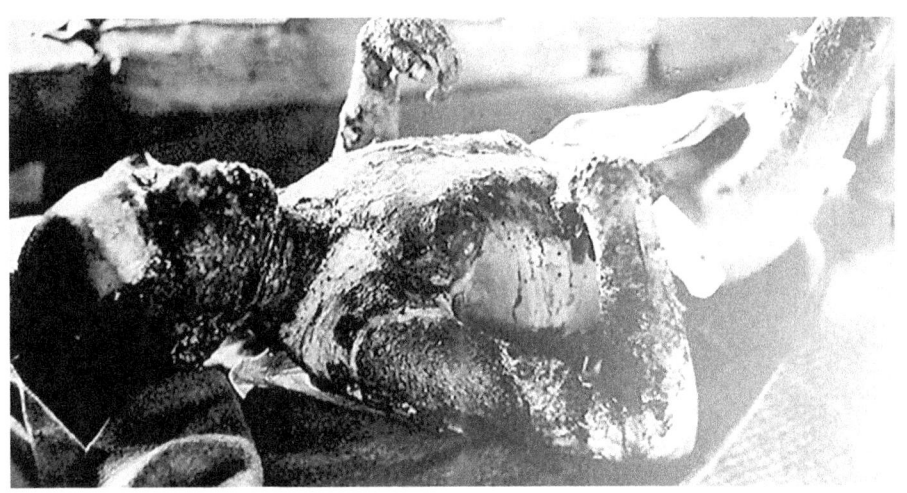

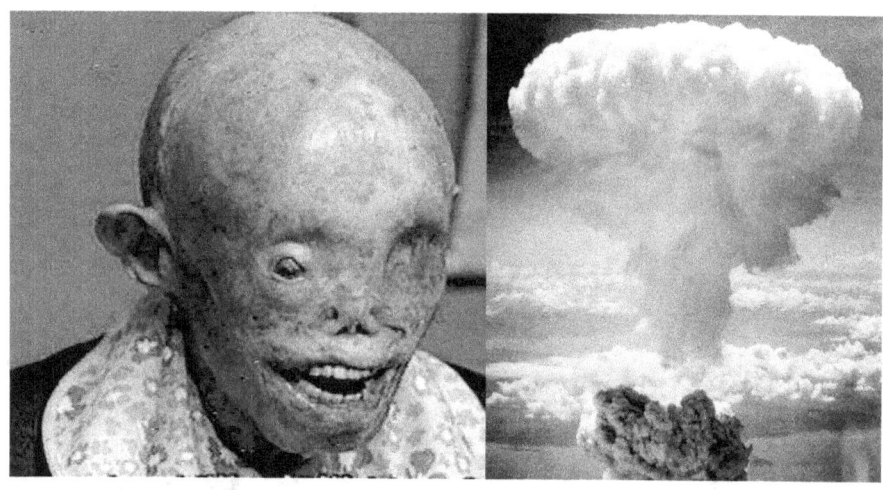

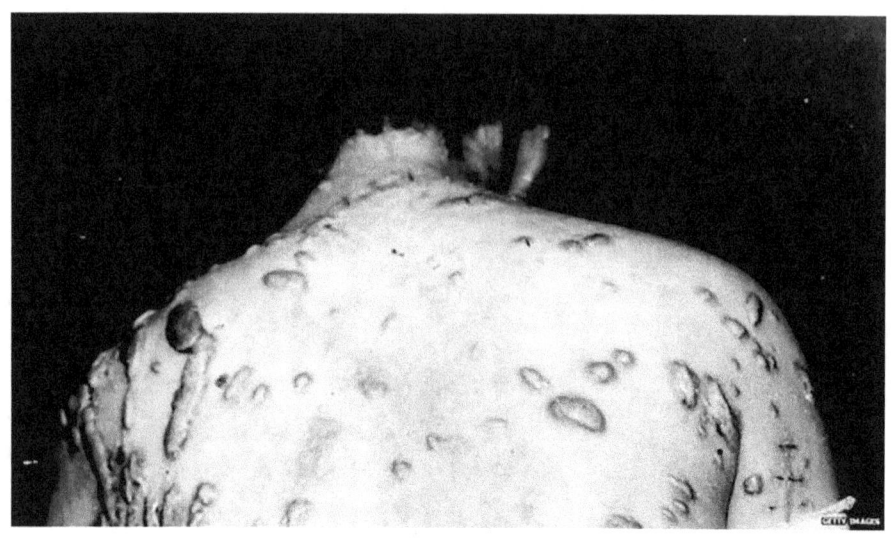

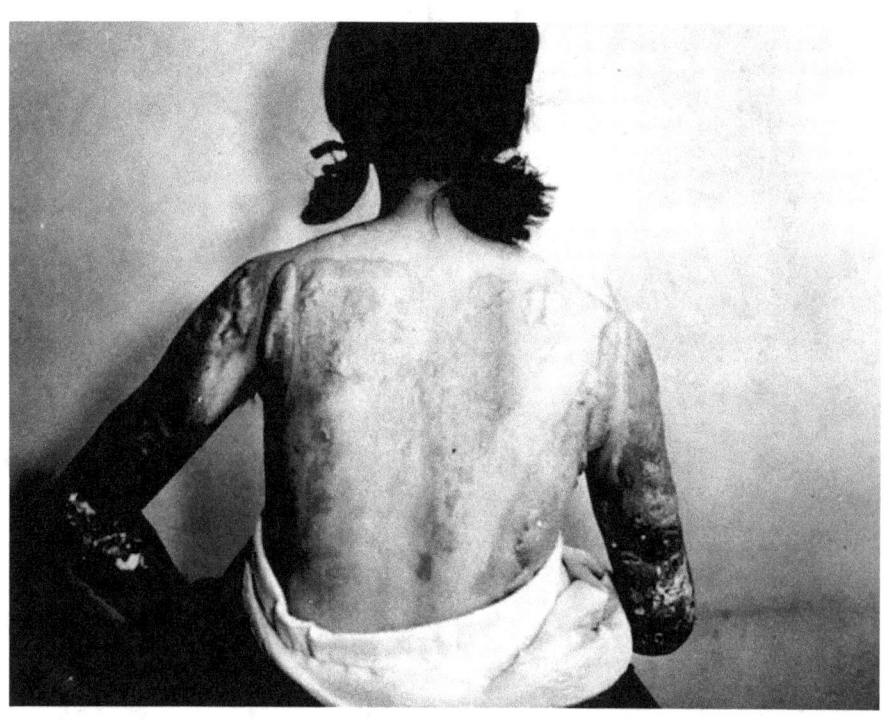

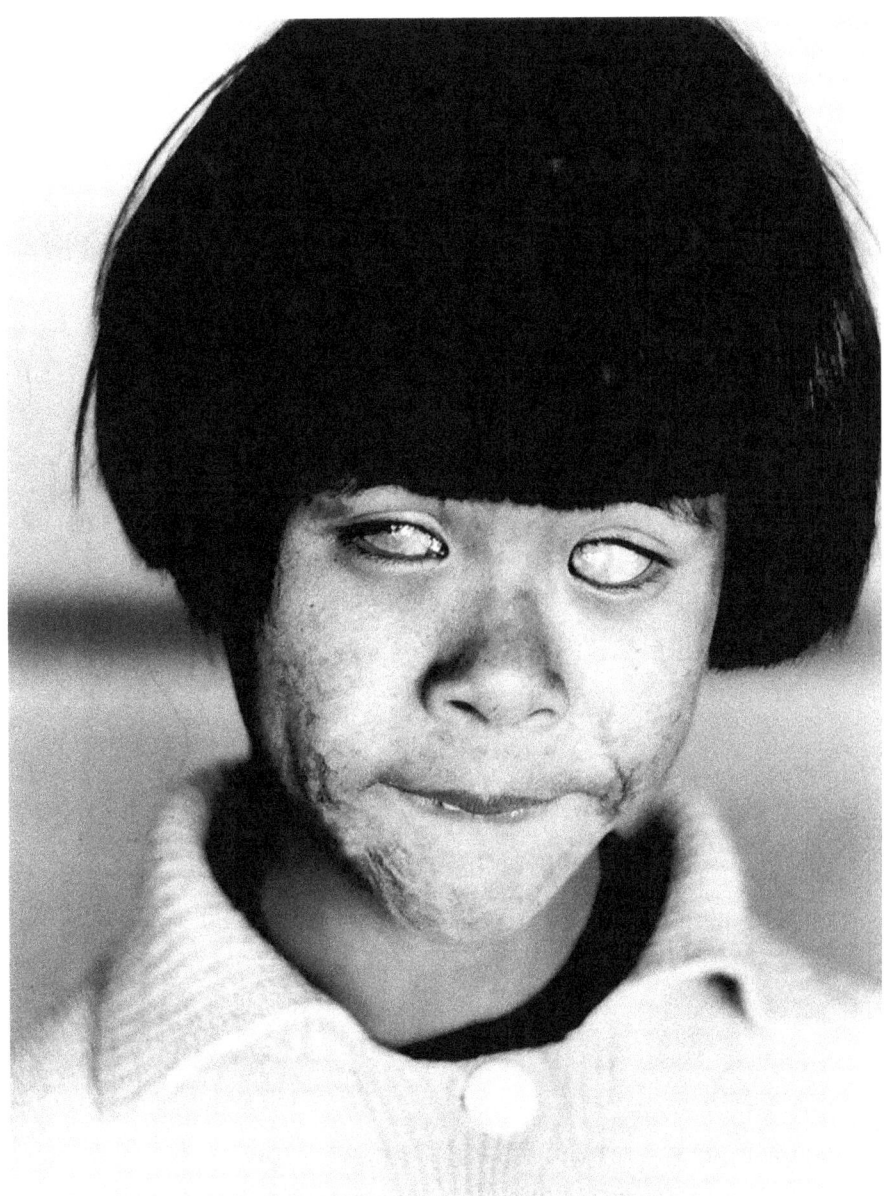

History's Closet

In Pearl Harbor
Japan permanently closed
2,335 sets of eyes

In Hiroshima and Nagasaki
We the people
Permanently closed between
100,000 and 200,000 sets of eyes

In history's closet
Many lessons we find
As Gandhi's truth reveals
"An eye for an eye
Makes our whole world blind"

History's closet
Reveals so much truth
Yet we adults
Still sacrifice our youth ~

Reflection Three

During one of my first graduate classes, when obtaining my master's in teaching, the professor provided the class an opportunity. He asked us to take 20 minutes of total silence to focus on and write something meaningful to us that we would like to share with the class. His purpose was two-fold as we were to recognize the value of silence and the importance of sharing ideas. The following poem, *A Precision Instrument*, was written during those 20 minutes. I have shared this poem in several other books as it has deep meaning to me.

~

A Percussion Instrument

A precision instrument
  dropped from the sky
It created a spark
  and an unceasing sickening cry

From a spark
  came a blinding light
  a monumental blinding flashbulb
  creating human silhouettes
  on concrete negatives

From a spark
  came hell's inferno
  a fire so hot
  only time
  could put it out

From a spark
  came shredded
  torn and melted
  human flesh
  as men, women, and children
  became running human torches
  searching for water

From a spark
 came a wind
 the strength of which
 the world
 had never seen

From a spark
 rose the ashes
 of silent
 incinerated
 families

From a spark
 cradled birth defects
 that linger on
 through generations

From a spark
 mushroomed crippling confusion
 that over 75 years later
 keeps generations
 and nations divided

From a spark
 came unanticipated pain
 unbelievable death
 and inconceivable destruction

From a spark
 of a precision instrument
 an instrument
 that still some proclaim
 propagates peace ~

Hiroshima shadows : When the atomic bomb was dropped on hiroshima the intensity of the blast was of such intensity that it permanently burned shadows of people and object into the ground. *Weird World*

@ weirdworldinsta

~

Reflection Four
Why?

While I was employed with the Department of Navy the excessive presence of America's nuclear arsenal played heavily on my mind. Why do we need to control our world through fear-filled threats? Wouldn't positive international leaderships be of greater benefit? How many mental health facilities, schools, hospitals, homes, places of employment, parks, highways, railroads, could be completely paid for with the funding utilized to design, construct, store, and potentially deploy these canisters of death? Think of the world poverty which could be eradicated if military funding was redirected.

Reflection Five
We Have the Answer

When thinking about Reflection Four, combining it with the COVID 19 pandemic, we need to add the fact that excessive funds currently spent on militarization, specifically nuclear weapons, could provide for the needs of our pandemic victims. Can you envision having the ability to fund pandemic needs for medical relief without political financial hesitation? Oh, what a relief it would be.

A silent aspect, in contrast between COVID 19 and a nuclear disaster, is the reality that during the pandemic we still have hospitals, adult care facilities, first responders, medical and science research facilities, grocery stores, supply chains, delivery capability, schools and churches to reopen. In a nuclear explosion, all would become contaminated dust. Even our air would be unbreathable.

This is reality. The COVID pandemic is treatable. A nuclear disaster is not. Each of our current nuclear bombs are 3,000 times as destructive as those we dropped on Hiroshima and Nagasaki.

Should one explode at Naval Base Kitsap, (formerly known as Naval Submarine Base Bangor) much of western Washington, if not the entire state, would become unlivable. With our prevailing west winds, combined with an unfathomable nuclear wind, much of the upper United States would quickly become contaminated. With numerous nuclear bombs stationed 20 air miles from Seattle, is it even possible to predict the chain reaction, should one nuclear weapon explode, perhaps exploding numerous others?

Is this survivable? Is this livable? This threat can be deactivated.

Reflection Six
Musical Messages

As children we are taught about "ownership" and what we must be willing to do as adults to protect what we own. A perfect example shines brightly in the often-favored song *"This Land is Your land."* The original words of this song repeatedly declare ownership. These words reinforce an environment in which we will go to extremes to protect what we own. These extremes reinforce militarism and private gun ownership. It is impossible to label the number of times I have heard men justify their weaponry ownership with the words "I need to be prepared if someone comes to rape my wife." How realistic is this fear-filled mentality? Below are the original verses of Woody Guthrie's song. When reading, think about what our ancestors did to possess and retain ownership of this land. How many were massacred, enslaved, and mistreated to gain and retain ownership of this land.

This Land Is Your Land
Written by Woody Guthrie

Refrain:

This land is your land, this land is my land
From California to the New York island,
From the redwood forest to the Gulf Stream waters;
This land was made for you and me.

1. As I was walking that ribbon of highway
   I saw above me that endless skyway;
   I saw below me that golden valley;
   This land was made for you and me.

Refrain:

2. I've roamed and rambled and I followed my footsteps
   To the sparkling sands of her diamond deserts;
   And all around me a voice was sounding;
   This land was made for you and me.

Refrain:

3. When the sun came shining, and I was strolling,
   And the wheat fields waving and the dust clouds rolling,
   As the fog was lifting a voice was chanting:
   This land was made for you and me.

Refrain:

4. As I went walking I saw a sign there,
   And on the sign it said "No Trespassing."
   But on the other side it didn't say nothing.
   That side was made for you and me.

Refrain:

5. In the shadow of the steeple I saw my people,
   By the relief office I seen my people;
   As they stood there hungry, I stood there asking
   Is this land made for you and me?

Refrain:

6. Nobody living can ever stop me,
   As I go walking that freedom highway;
   Nobody living can ever make me turn back
   This land was made for you and me.

Notice, that later versions of this song omitted the 4th and 6th verses which focus on private property ownership.

When focusing on our call to love one another and the moral value of welcoming a stranger, do the song's words encourage or discourage acceptance of others? Does our value of sharing and caring for others come through? Are these words focusing on ownership or unity?

For years, the song *"This Land is Your Land"* has echoed through my mind, reverberating concerns as to our nation's attitudes toward unity and acceptance of others. Finally, after years of mental bouncing, I sat peacefully listening to my inner concerns. Through this process the following song flowed forth. My desire is to focus on gratitudinal unity, "one nation under God, with liberty and justice for all."

Our Obligation

This land's not your land, this land's not my land
From the torch of freedom to the rainbowed islands
From the Artic Ocean to Key West motion
This land is leased to you and me

The original tenants are oh so right
Heaven's Spirit owns all in sight
For Mother Earth where we do stride
It's up to us to care with pride
For this land is leased to you and me

From heaven's Landlord to our circling seashore
We're tasked with grooming earth's floor and more
Through unified rhythm and vocal accord
Our gentle actions can produce much more

Inalienable rights once gifted to all
Nowhere mentions constructing a wall
Our obligation is to respect each other
Each and every sister and brother

As sharing hands stretch across blessed lands
Life is rising from watered sands
As the fires of freedom gently warm each heart
It's our obligation to grant equal starts

For this land's not your land, this land's not my land
Our obligation is to understand
Our Landlord's desire is we aspire
To elevate unity higher and higher

Heaven is guiding as we look and listen
As peaceful waters begin to glisten
The task is ours to nourish all
As we respond to heaven's call

This land's not your land this land's not my land
From the torch of freedom to the rainbowed islands
From the Artic Ocean to Key West motion
This land is leased to you and me

This land is leased to you and me ~

It is my hope that we, as one nation under God, will join our mindsets
in being more grateful and thankful for the gifts God has blessed each of
us with, as we become more willing to share these blessings with earthly
family members.

Chapter Three
Hope Lives

Getty Image, Hiroshima a year after the atomic bomb,
showing government-supplied wooden buildings
built on the flattened city.

Lesson takes place in a bomb-damaged classroom in Hiroshima in 1946, while thousands of bodies were still buried under the ruins. Getty Images.

Reflection Seven
My Gardening Reality

An enjoyable portion of my life has been spent nurturing gardens. Through this process, I have arrived at the realization that human life is quite comparable to gardening. In the cycle of life, infants emerge from darkness. Following a period of sharing their beauty, individuals are buried only to raise and bloom in a new, heavenly environment. During this process new flower seeds, also rooted in darkness, bloom forth entering radiant family bouquets. This is a simplified comparison as we humans have free wills and decisions to make, if and when we choose to make them.

For years, hidden in my damp mental ground, many serious concerns periodically raised their hand bidding for the daylight of attention, meekly saying, "I'm still here and I do care." Throwing some compost on these thoughts many have remain dormant. Tucked deep inside my dark depths, a serious concern silently sleeps as its roots spread throughout my extremities. An alarming concern which others may also suppress in mental dormancy. If my concern is publicly shared, will it become noticed, or simply indifferently blend with my garden's seasonal red lucifer flowers?

Oh, how I wish millions would recognize the danger hidden in political compost. Deceptive compost phrased as "strategic stability," "our deterrence" our second-strike capability," camouflages the fact that today's nuclear weapons are 3,000 times as deadly as the atomic bombs we dropped on Hiroshima and Nagasaki. Bombs that turned human flesh into ashes, or flaming human torches, screaming as they hopelessly ran for unavailable water. Intentionally camouflaged, these realities deliberately distract our citizenry from reality. Lucifer blooms are bright red, drawing our attention from other attractive realities living in the garden. Perhaps there is a parallel here, as our government's comfortable, red hot, attractive nuclear security blanket camouflages our individual, national, and international desires for the beauty hope delivers. In a nuclear war, life as we know it, will be extremely short-lived. By the elimination of nuclear weapons, life can bloom brightly.

Nuclear weapons, in concordance with the United Nations Treaty on the Prohibition of Nuclear Weapons, (TPNW), became illegal as of January 22, 2021. Nuclear nations now have a calling to walk through the United Nations open door. Has our government intentionally buried this information in our congressional garden? If so, perhaps we, the gardeners, can nurture its visibility.

Red Lucifer flowers

Pleasure Is to Share

Our world's true happiness
Is not delivered from a store

A beach walk refreshes
Our soul
But total joy
Is not on the shore

Love's not in a drink
No matter what we pour

Joy is not on a shelf
Or tucked
In some secret drawer

It is not the clothes
Or jewelry we adore

Happiness is not a thing,
No matter what
Thing we bring

True pleasure is to share
Showing we care ~

~

Oh So True

His message
could not be more true

As when on His cross Christ said
"Father, forgive them
for they know not
what they do"

It was so appropriate then
and today remains oh so true

As those who follow deceit
Truly
know not
what they do

But the fact we are all
one forgiving family
is oh so true ~

~

Shh, Mom is Speaking

Mom's message quite clear
Nuclear weapons
Cause fear
I do not hold them dear

No matter
How you justify
With my survival
They do not comply

I know my heavens
Can become quite wicked
Perhaps the result
Of chemicals uplifted

Periodically
My ground does shake
Because chemical injections
Make my belly ache

These same injected chemicals
That make me quake
Make my ground water unsafe
For human intake

Furthermore
Is this proposal
My oceans are not
A garbage disposal

Shh
Please listen to your Mom
Life can be beautiful
Sweet and calm

As your Mother Earth
Who gave life birth
Please listen to heaven's Father
Who gave earth birth

Love one another
And care for your Mother
For currently
You have no other ~

~

Seize the Moment

COVID 19
Came on our scene
Threatening so much
But not everything

First responders
And communication needs
Regulated stores to shop
But not, our well-used coffee pot

Sure, there was stress
But it calls for each
To seize the moment
To nourish and teach

A teachable moment
Has made itself quite clear
Nuclear weapons
Are no longer, are illegal here

A pandemic's pain
Will soon heal
Our earth's survival
A nuclear war will steal

"The Treaty to Prohibit Nuclear Weapons"
(TPNW)
Was ratified by the United Nations,
As of January 22, 2021
Nuclear weapons are now illegal
On God's earthly creation

The decision is made
The myth now exposed
Nuclear weapons
Are too deadly to hold

Our time is now
To take a stand
Together we can
Remove nukes
From our land

To our congress elected
Communications is our channel
Encouraging nuclear weapons
To be dismantled

Justification
Lives in the fact
From used nuclear weapons
There's no coming back ~

Reflection Eight
Moral Decisions

While considering my options, prior to resigning my civil service position with the Navy, discussions with spirit filled individuals provided insight. One individual was the Catholic chaplain at Bangor. During one of our conversations, he shared an experience deeply concerning him. The chaplain had selected one Eucharistic Minister for each of the submarines stationed at the base. Prior to departing on extended cruises, each minister would receive a set number of consecrated hosts dependent upon the extent of their deployment. Upon the sub's return each Eucharistic Minister would return the exact number of hosts they departed with. This not only indicated that no one had received communion at a service, but that the minister himself did not even receive communion. This occurred regularly on every submarine. The Father's explanation was, "perhaps Christ does not want to be received on a nuclear submarine".

This was one of many factors convincing me that I did not want to provide for our family with money related to our potential doomsday destruction. The base chaplain also resigned his commission at Bangor, honoring his moral convictions.

~

The Cuban Crisis

Once I believed
That war was just
As a child, nightly prayers
For my brother in Korea
Became our family must

Then came the Cuban Crisis
Which I will never forget
Our Air Force base became
A nuclear launch pad
America's most massive yet

Loaded B-52s
Lined the flight line
Cuba and our southeast
Soon to be
Radiated dust left behind

But President Kennedy
Wanted war no more
To diplomacy
He forced open the door

His words sincere
Made it quite clear,
No nuclear weapons
Our world would smear

Ingrained in my mind
Words or weapons
JFK's diplomacy
Peace did define

But those in power
In our military elite
Preferred a nuclear war
Desiring enemies to defeat

Not getting their way
They planed the day
When and how
They would eliminate
JFK

The same mindset
Smolders still
Ignoring the youth-filled coffins
War still does fill

So, what's our justification
To retain nuclear weapons
When we know quite well
They will turn our world
Into one fiery hell ~

~

Reflection Nine
Political Participation

Issues, including automatic, semi-automatic weapons and nuclear weapons, and discrimination have been tabled far too long. Some people refuse to talk about them, saying, "I can't do anything about it so why try? Many governments depend upon this indifferent mindset. These issues provide a means to threaten, inflict harm, and produce the death of many innocent individuals. So why do we refuse to discuss such destructive capability? Have we been taught that it is ok live in fear? Fear is what military industrialists use to control and promote the use of weapons.

The truth is we are one human family, living on one common earth to which one God breathed life. Our commonalities are far more prevalent than our differences. Internally we desire and deserve to live in peace. Peace for ourselves. Peace for our families. Peace for our communities, churches, and nations. With this desire in mind, perhaps our current path needs to lead toward this desired lifestyle.

We do have differences, but it has been stated "variety is the spice of life." So, let's spice up our lives with political and social peace discussions. Let's enjoy life together as we share ideas aimed at reducing bickering. We are God's children, and our Father is telling us to behave. Are we listening?

With all sincerity, I believe our current social infection can be healed. In tackling issues resulting in violence, life can refocus on prosperous pathways of healing, as we move forward. Hope does smile.

The following quote from "*JFK and the Unspeakable*," by James W. Douglass, provides insight, shedding a steady light, on achieving peace. Nowhere have I found a more realistic approach to unity. The following was delivered by President John F. Kennedy as a portion of his commencement speech at American University, June 10, 1963.

President John F. Kennedy –
American University - June 10, 1963

"What kind of peace do I mean? What kind of peace do we seek? Not a Pax Americana enforced on the world by American weapons of war. Not the peace of the grave or the security of the slave. I am talking about genuine peace, the kind that makes life on earth worth living, the kind that enables men and nations to grow and to hope and to build a better life for their children—not merely peace for Americans but peace for all men and women—not merely in our time but peace for all time."

Personal Experience
Eielson AFB – Fairbanks, Alaska
November 22, 1963

I was stationed at Eielson Air Force Base, 25 miles south of Fairbanks, Alaska. Having finished a 16-hour night shift, I went to bed. It was my 21st birthday and we planned to party that evening. I was looking forward to some fun. I was sound asleep when my friend Gerald woke me up. I had never seen him so troubled as he fearfully blurted out, "President

Kennedy has been shot, we are on alert." Not wanting to believe him, I turned on the radio. We received the Armed Services Network and sure enough, Gerald was telling the truth.

Having watched President Kennedy's leadership through the Cuban crisis, I was fully aware Kennedy had established enemies in high-ranking military officials. Immediately, I believed this was an inside job. Many of our leaders were unbelievably disappointed when, through Kennedy's leadership, Russia backed off. I had witnessed countless bombers fueled and armed, ready to annihilate Cuba, with no realization by military officials such massive bombing would have eliminated a large portion of life as we know it on Mother Earth. It was obvious many military had their finger on Armageddon's trigger. I was convinced President Kennedy saved our world, and for this, he was assassinated. The book "*JFK And The Unspeakable*," by James W. Douglass, sheds a believable light on President Kennedy's wisdom and his assassination.

President John F. Kennedy – American University - June 10, 1963

"Let us focus instead on a more practical, more attainable peace—based not on sudden revolution in human nature but on a gradual evolution in human institutions—on a series of concrete actions and affective agreements which are in the interest of all concerned. There is no single, simple key to this peace—no grand or magic formula to be adopted by one or two powers. Genuine peace must be the product of many nations, the sum of many acts. It must be dynamic, not static, changing to meet the challenge of each new generation. For peace is a process—a way of solving problems."

Personal Experiences

Standing for peace is not easy, believe me I know that quite well. Doing so, however, is quite fulfilling. The following experiences I have not shared before as I do not want to scare nonviolent supporters away.

However, the truth has a way of rising above fear. The following are a few experiences which influenced my desire to speak out. Upon resigning my civil service position alternative employment was essential for our family of five. Fortunately, Jerrie, while attending college full time, also found employment. Her supportive endurance was, and remains, incredible.

To begin in open honesty, the entire process took a heavy toll on each member of our family. The years included five moves. Our first move involved several garage sales which included the children selling some of their favored toys. New schools and friendships for our children were difficult transitions. Relocating from a rural half-acre with a two-story home, to a city environment and a two-bedroom apartment was sever. I am sure many of you understand the results of extended unemployment. Jerrie was, and remains our family anchor, holding us together.

Immediately, following my resignation, each morning as I left for the employment office, or to apply for a job, I was followed by naval security. A shiny, government licensed car pulling out behind you is impossible to miss. Especially when the two agents are wearing suits and ties. I did not have knowledge of any secret military information, so why are they so paranoid? Why pay the salaries of two agents for several weeks to simply drive around or sit in a parking lot? What a waste of our taxes. The answer is simple--as our military forces fear someone may speak the truth about the dangers of nuclear weapons.

It quickly became visible that I would never find employment in the immediate military community, so my search expanded to Seattle. To begin with, I selected three well-known employment agencies and visited all three of them. At each agency I filled out their application submitting it along with my resume to each interviewer I spoke with. I also received their business card for future contacts. Several days later, after not receiving any phone calls, I called each one. Having their card, I was connected directly to each person. Amazingly, each representative gave me the same feedback "I'm sorry, we have no record of you in our files". Two added, "I don't recall speaking with you, and I do not have your application." Blacklisting is illegal in the United States, but I can assure you it happens.

After my yearlong search for employment, our family moved from Silverdale to an apartment in Kirkland, just east of Seattle. One day I arrived home shortly after our children had gotten home from school. Surprisingly, two naval security officers were in our apartment questioning our two sons. It was obvious this was harassment, as what they were asking could not have involved my boys. The timing of the occurrence in Silverdale was weeks after we had moved to Kirkland. When I pointed that out, they left.

After a short time, I obtained a maintance job at an apartment complex. Periodically, I would speak at public functions which led to our home phone being tapped. It was totally ridiculous, but government paranoia breeds the ridiculous.

After a couple more family moves and more stable employment, we were able to buy a home. With stability, I joined Veterans for Peace. I can't say for sure there was a connection, but varied vehicles would randomly park on the street beside our home. One time, after our youngest was in college, Jerrie and I returned home to find her computer unplugged and our bathroom exhaust fan cover hanging from the ceiling.

One fall, with damp, cold northwest weather, a new Mercedes convertible would periodically park across the street directly in front of our home. The top was down, even though it was cold. The driver enjoyed periodically staring into our living room window. After several weeks, one Saturday Jerrie and I were leaving to go grocery shopping a couple miles from our home. His car was parked facing east. We left heading west. As we were walking from our car to the store, the man drove directly past us. How did he even know where we were headed? I had not seen him following us.

In October 2008, a couple days after I had diligently weeded and groomed our gardens, I spotted a fresh large lump of dirt in the garden near our gate. As I raked the top off, a pistol appeared. Not wanting my prints on it I picked it up with a stick. After some deliberation, I called the county sheriff. The weapon, a 9 MM handgun, had been stolen from an apartment complex about 15 miles from here. So, what's the connection? I will never know. However, the Mercedes convertible never returned.

These events are shared so you may understand the paranoia our government thrives on. This paranoia, however unnerving, is not life threatening. Nuclear weapons are.

~

The following copied and pasted quotes are excerpts taken directly from Vladimir Putin's Jan. 27, 2021 presentation to the united Nations.

Vladimir Putin - Jan. 27, 2021
United Nations

"Of course, such a heated global conflict is impossible in principle, I hope. This is what I am pinning my hopes on, because this would be the end of humanity. However, as I have said, the situation could take an unexpected and uncontrollable turn--unless we do something to prevent this."

***

"Colleagues, despite this tangle of differences and challenges, we certainly should keep a positive outlook on the future and remain committed to a constructive agenda. It would be naive to come up with universal miraculous recipes for resolving the above problems. But we certainly need to try to work out common approaches, bring our positions as close as possible and identify sources that generate global tensions."

***

"Once again, I want to emphasise my thesis that accumulated socioeconomic problems are the fundamental reason for unstable global growth"

"So, the key question today is how to build a programme of actions in order to not only quickly restore the global and national economies affected by the pandemic, but to ensure that this recovery is sustainable in the long run, relies on a high-quality structure and helps overcome the burden of social imbalances. Clearly, with the above restrictions and macroeconomic policy in mind, economic growth will largely rely on fiscal incentives with state budgets and central banks playing the key role."

***

"Actually, we can see these kinds of trends in the developed countries and also in some developing economies as well. An increasing role of the state in the socioeconomic sphere at the national level obviously implies greater responsibility and close interstate interaction when it comes to issues on the global agenda."

"Calls for inclusive growth and for creating decent standards of living for everyone are regularly made at various international forums. This is how it should be, and this is an absolutely correct view of our joint efforts."

"It is clear that the world cannot continue creating an economy that will only benefit a million people, or even the golden billion. This is a destructive precept. This model is unbalanced by default. The recent developments, including migration crises, have reaffirmed this once again."

"We must now proceed from stating facts to action, investing our efforts and resources into reducing social inequality in individual countries and into gradually balancing the economic development standards of different countries and regions in the world. This would put an end to migration crises."

"The essence and focus of this policy aimed at ensuring sustainable and harmonious development are clear. They imply the creation of new opportunities for everyone, conditions under which everyone will be able to develop and realise their potential regardless of where they were born and are living."

"I would like to point out four key priorities, as I see them. This might be old news, but since Klaus has allowed me to present Russia's position, my position, I will certainly do so."

First, everyone must have comfortable living conditions, including housing and affordable transport, energy and public utility infrastructure. Plus environmental welfare, something that must not be overlooked.

"Second, everyone must be sure that they will have a job that can ensure sustainable growth of income and, hence, decent standards of living. Everyone must have access to an effective system of lifelong education, which is absolutely indispensable now and which will allow people to develop, make a career and receive a decent pension and social benefits upon retirement."

"Third, people must be confident that they will receive high-quality and effective medical care whenever necessary, and that the national healthcare system will guarantee access to modern medical services."

"Fourth, regardless of the family income, children must be able to receive a decent education and realise their potential. Every child has potential."

"This is the only way to guarantee the cost-effective development of the modern economy, in which people are perceived as the end, rather than the means. Only those countries capable of attaining progress in at least these four areas will facilitate their own sustainable and all-inclusive development. These areas are not exhaustive, and I have just mentioned the main aspects."

***

"The reality is such that really different development centres with their distinctive models, political systems and public institutions have taken shape in the world. Today, it is very important to create mechanisms for harmonising their interests to prevent the diversity and natural competition of the development poles from triggering anarchy and a series of protracted conflicts.

To achieve this we must, in part, consolidate and develop universal institutions that bear special responsibility for ensuring stability and security in the world and for formulating and defining the rules of conduct both in the global economy and trade."

***

"Only together can we achieve progress in resolving such critical problems as global warming, the reduction of forestlands, the loss of biodiversity, the increase in waste, the pollution of the ocean with plastic and so on, and find an optimal balance between economic development and the preservation of the environment for the current and future generations".

***

~

We are well aware of the current displeasure of the Russian citizens, however insights into President Putin, as shared above, may provide insight into his desire to make positive political alterations to calm his citizenry. Now is the opportune moment for United States leaders and Russian leaders to communicate. This may be a long-awaited window of opportunity our world has been hoping and praying for.

World Peace
Is our world's life insurance policy,
Which we all
Must invest in ~

Chapter Four
Change

Pixabay

It's Within Our Reach

Peace is not displayed
As red or blue,
It is displayed through the actions
Of me and you

So, for heaven's sake,
The God we're under
Needs not hear
Our angry thunder

And here on earth
Our children acquire
Their deep desire
To happily
Rise a bit higher

These children learn
From our adult actions.
What lesson are we teaching
As their main attraction

So, what is it
That makes America great?
Is it our ability to share
Democracy's common plate

If so, it is within
Our reach
To serve and practice
What we teach ~

~

An Eye for An Eye

I know for many
This is hard to believe
And for some
Unable to conceive

As children we were taught
Not to hit back
As adults some prefer
To provide no slack

As history teaches
The message so clear
Violence promotes violence
Promoting anger, pain, and fear

As we travel
Thorough the ages
There is a spiritual lesson
On those historical pages

"An eye for an eye
Makes the whole world blind"
Gandhi's advice
His message sublime

From whom
Was Gandhi's wisdom derived,
Christ's final instruction
Luke 23:34 remains alive

Christ, nailed to our cross
By those in authority
Made forgiveness
His final priority

"Father forgive them
For they know not what they do"
As He forgave his crucifiers
And each me and you

Jesus not only
Commands us to forgive
But to the criminal who confessed
In heaven he would live

God's Son's final instruction
Was to forgive

Christ's final action
Was to forgive

"An eye for an eye
Makes the whole world blind"

What is the example
We wish
To leave behind ~

~

Reflection Ten
What We Stand For

**Hope's smile
is deceptive
on the face of the deceiver**

**Hope sincerely smiles
on the face
of the believer ~**

As a 78-year-old cradle Catholic, who spent three years in a Catholic high school, it is difficult to believe today's divide in the Catholic Church. Having been taught to love one another, I cannot help but wonder what has split these once treasured Christian values.

In 2016 Donald Trump received 52% of the Catholic vote, and a large percentage of the overall Christian vote. A man who smiled about grabbing young Miss America pageant contestants between their legs; who filed bankruptcy on his constructed hotels to avoid paying contractors – who in turn could not pay their employees, resulting is an extended food line near his empty bankrupt Atlantic City Taj Mahal (which Jerrie and I witnessed); who discriminates at every opportunity; who lies, cheats, steals, and misleads, actually captured Christian hearts, minds, and souls, along with their trust, so he could pick his supporters' pockets, while driving painful wedges in families. Amazingly, he smiled while doing so. Normally, a smile displays pleasure. Trump's deep pleasure, through his discrimination and deception, makes him smile all the way to the bank. Still unbelievably high numbers of Christians voted for him the second time around.

What is disheartening is so many Christians supported his dishonesty based primarily on the single issue of abortion. It mattered not that

Donald Trump had entirely aborted all moral values and his stand on abortion was a political ploy used to pick potential voter pockets. The end result revealed to me how Hitler may have swayed so many to believe his deadly deception. It is difficult to believe how vulnerable so many can be.

~

Reflection Eleven
Change

Our world, our nation, and our faith life are currently in massive transition. The current difference, between evolutionary change and now, is our worldly pandemic and deeply-rooted political differences. This stress-filled survival is universally shared, as we are all in this together. The social struggles of one culture impacts the struggles of all others. As a world, we are medically, socially, educationally, and spiritually in transition as we travel from the mindset of national independence to worldly interdependency.

On a small personal scale, when making a move, I've found there is a four-fold process. Individuals, couples, and families, desiring change, first recognize where they are, why they are moving, their destination, and the means to arrive at that destination.

Triggering the desire for change on a national level are numerous common dissatisfactions with our current stress-filled lifestyles. We may not all be in a physical relocation mode; however, we are unified in our mental and spiritual transitions. With COVID 19, political and religious differences, combined with the natural maturing and aging process, change is frequently desired. How we address this conversion will determine how mutually livable our worldly home becomes.

For me, this transitional process has mentally surfaced for years, but recently was spotlighted while I was re-landscaping our backyard. Hopefully, I can make this comparison relatable and more understandable.

For the past 30+ years, our small backyard has been potluckly landscaped. With no final plan, plants were deposited wherever they fit. A portion of this is related to my desire for a waterfall which has been changed at least four times. My know-better landscaping background constantly spoke differently, but I planted out of quick necessity. As a result, our backyard turned out quite messy.

A plan for a garden makeover was mandatory. I needed to decide which plants would be replaced or relocated and to where. I needed to stop discriminating against the beautiful plants by hiding them against the fence and bring them forward, highlighting their beauty. During the process weedy weapons needed to be composted. Afterall, weeds add seeds while adding no beauty. By relocating a variety of evergreen ferns from a local nursery, (coincidentally named Flower World) to our garden, an evergreen background will accent the forward plants. The front of the garden now has lower growing multicolored primroses which joyfully bloom in partial sunlight. Other plants are now blended in clusters.

As for the water fountain, our current one provides varied levels where birds can both drink and bathe. With a variety of bird feeders, supported by an arbor, our garden receives many welcomed guests. The peanut feeder for Steller jays and crows also attracts squirrels, and neighborhood bunnies' munch on some of the lower plants. All are welcome. Our backyard is a fun oasis. With birds enjoying the fountain, the necessity to flush out some their undesirable droppings is a given. Although not always pleasant, flushing, like weeding, is an essential part of gardening. During summer months a relaxing hammock provides comfortable maps.

Comparing a small backyard to a nation may not be totally relatable; however, if peace is to bloom on any scale, it starts at home. We need to compost excessive weedy weapons so we can focus on an unthreatened human garden. Life, as plants, survive when nourished with love. Love, in turn, regenerates live.

The choice is ours. What values do we choose to plant in our children's gardens?

~

Reflection Twelve
Steps Toward Peace

Peace is a universal human desire. Sometimes we share this yearning, but all too often we shelve it for later discussion. Coupled with this, exists an "accept what is" attitude which leads to a status quo, limiting progress. These attitudes need to change. We cannot wait, hoping someday peace will self-bloom. Blooming, requires grooming. Unattended gardens produce undesirable weeds, ending up with an undesirable chaos.

If we truly desire to achieve peace, we must acknowledge where we are at and develop a workable peace plan. Recipes, when followed, can produce delicious results. Some recipes, achieved in layers, consist of several steps . A cake recipe may have separate filling and frosting recipes. Creative applications can produce delicious results. We also have recipes developed by adaptations to meet varied desires of our final creation. With these factors in mind, the following recipe may be creatively adapted to achieve more desirable results. However, currently we have only sparse piecemeal plans, most of which are verbal. Whatever the finalized Peace Progress Recipe becomes, the following is a solid plan to achieve peace on many levels.

Peace Process Steps

Step One: Firearms Reductions

1-A. Critical to a potential peace process requires a series of meetings between international leaders who set and establish the stage. Initially, the process should involve the presidents of Russia and the US with a series of discussions through which they establish joint understanding, on mutual and individual needs, while establishing desires and boundaries. Paths may join at intersections and separate according to national perimeters, with disarmament the agreed upon platform. China should be added on a path toward the United Nations.

1-A. a. Balancing the process, joint meetings with several national leaders can evolve through well attended United Nations assemblies.

1-A. b. Critical, and complimentary, to this process is to include our world's wealthy advantaged. Unity between those who control our world's wealth and weapons is essential.

1-A. c. Religious considerations, combined spiritual fertilizer, are crucial to provide heavenly harmony. Spiritual considerations and guidelines are essential to any peace process.

1-B. While Step One is evolving, extensive education of the public about the necessity to removing automatic and semi-automatic weapons is appropriately provided to all ages. Information presented should be based on the unnecessary and dangerous aspects of these weapons. Additionally, the need for target practicing and hunting. Hunting is a sport, not a massacre. Weapons contribute to the escalation of violence and mass murders. Automatic and semi-automatic weapons also increase the necessity for law enforcement to escalate their weapons, leading to an unlivable spiral.

This process needs to be gentle, informative, age related, and believable. It will take time, because to rush through the educational process will produce a crumbling foundation. Special care is to be used to avoid instilling fear, or panic, at all age levels.

1-C. The enactment of federal laws, making it illegal to design, develop, distribute, import, exchange, possess, trade, or sell automatic and semi-automatic weapons and related ammunition, for non-governmental military use is our essential foundation. Breaking these laws will result in severe penalties, fines, or possible imprisonment.

1-D. Prior to the activation of the law regarding automatic and semi-automatic weapons, each state and territory needs to immediately develop and enact a plan to achieve and adhere to the federal law established by Step 1- C in a safe and responsible manner. Recycling will be an important and necessary part of our weapons reduction plan.

1-E. The actual process of deactivating, disarming, dismantling, and recycling of such weapons and ammunition will take place at safe facilities to ensure staff and public safety. The recycled weapons may include other assaultive items individuals or organizations may wish to donate.

1-F. The accomplishment of steps toward our unified peace needs to be recognized and celebrated. Goals, when accomplished, need celebrating.

Step Two: Celebrating Success

2-A. Local, and state, Peace Progress Parties, celebrating the recycling of automatic and semi-automatic weapons, along with their ammunitions, will be established. These celebrations will take place in designated, nonprofit, government-owned and operated facilities and may include food, potlucks, games, playgrounds, nonalcoholic drinks, dancing, or whatever the participating communities choose and plan. Due to environmental concerns, fireworks will not be allowed at these celebrations. Also the locations will be separate from the dismantling and recycling facilities to provide for public safety.

Step Three: Nuclear Arms Elimination

3-A. Firearms removal education explaining and justifying the removal of nuclear weapons will be implemented. The educational process shell be developed and delivered accordingly to all age levels. Special care will be used to avoid instilling fear or panic at all age levels. Justification for such action exists through our United Nations enactment of the TPNW on January 22, 2021, making nuclear weapons illegal.

Our United States is tasked with recognizing and honoring the United Nations Treaty on the Prohibition of Nuclear Weapons (TPNW), established December 4, 2017, which became effective January 22, 2021. Nuclear weapons are now illegal and the responsibility to implement this is in the hands of our citizenry. TPNW was signed by 122 of the 193 member nations. Its implementation depends upon citizen involvement to activate government action. Our inaction is no longer a solution.

Perhaps a persuasive tactic to encourage universal participation in nuclear disarmament could be the 122 complying nations' refusal to trade with nonparticipating nations.

3-B. Steps One and Two address the promotion of individual and group nonviolence. Step Three focuses on eliminating national and international self-destruction. If life on Mother Earth is to survive, we must listen to the voice of our Father and Creator, calling us to love one another. Perhaps the connections between Mother Earth, our Father Creator, and humanity can be viewed as our "trinity for survival."

3-C. As shown on the following chart, presently contaminated nuclear waste is deposited in 80 sites throughout our United States.

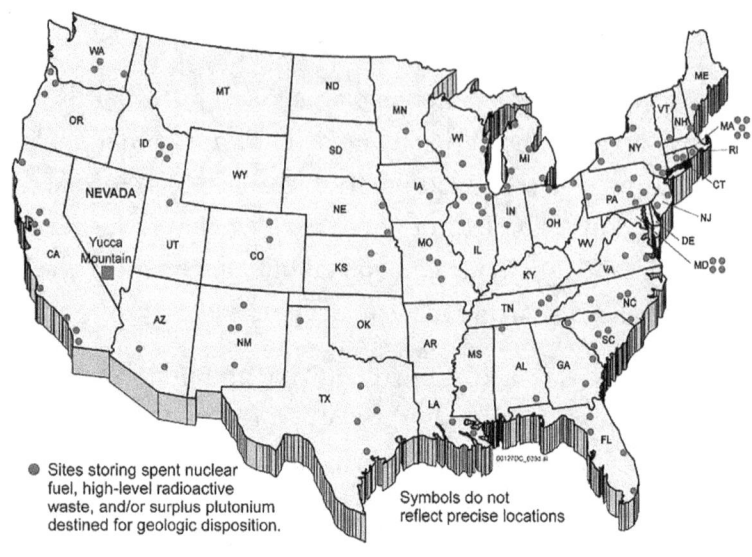

Sites storing spent nuclear fuel, high-level radioactive waste, and/or surplus plutonium destined for geologic disposition.

Symbols do not reflect precise locations

Nuclear weapons
Are not a safe gimmick
Reality reveals they are
A sleeping pandemic
Totally untreatable
By any medic ~

There is no safe way to store, recycle, or safely control the hazardous waste we already have. As we continue building more explosive weapons, we have no way to safely protect our citizens from this waste. Does this make sense? On a smaller, less hazardous scale, if we have a broken sewer pipe in the basement which contains our food storage for our first-floor restaurant, do we continue using and flushing the toilets on the upper levels of this 100-story hotel? Let's get real! We can now destroy our world hundreds, if not thousands, of times over. So what are we doing to prevent self-destruction? Develop, build, and deploy more deadly self-annihilation? Wow!!! Is this not a dangerously self-destructive way to live.

Do we have a plan to address and reverse this?

Years ago, I listened to an idea which, after years of consideration, still appears solid. Our sun consists of continual nuclear explosions. Would it be feasible to manufacture extra-long-range missiles, load them with nuclear waste, and launch them toward the sun? The sun's extreme heat would quite likely destroy it long before it reached the sun. We can try a practice missile--without nuclear waste, as a trial experiment.

Think about this. Continuing on the path we are on **will lead to self-destruction**. We need to stop all design and construction of nuclear weaponry and actually deal with nuclear waste. Once, and only after nuclear weaponry production has **permanently stopped**, we could try delivering nuclear waste toward the sun. Our children deserve better than to continue living in fear of self-annihilation.

3-C Repair international relations as we celebrate nuclear liberation.

Chapter Five
Hope Shines

Photo of Lake Washington by Jerrie Drinkwine

Reflection Thirteen
One Human Family

A large portion of our military force is developed under the disguise of *might makes right*. To use these weapons, many of our youth become disposable pawns, trained, and armed to control or eliminate an enemy. Sometimes a self-made enemy. As a result of our might makes right deception, uncountable loved ones become militarily sacrificed by those in power to protect the profits of weapons manufactures. According to the U.S. Department of State, our government manages about $55 billion per year in the sales of defense equipment. Is this defense industry what our youth are actually protecting?

Historically, this approach has destroyed nations, massacred cities and villages, and filled cemeteries with the bodies of our children, all under the might makes right mentality. Recently, this mentality was allowed to tweet and fuel violence from our White House, while inciting violence and death throughout our nation. This *might makes right* attitude exploded on January 6, 2021, as radicals seized the U.S. Capitol. If this mentality continues, what does our future hold? How militarized do we the people allow our nation to become? How many weapons do we need to self-destruct?

When reflecting on our Creator's creation, we know that from the origin of life we have been called to respect nature and to "Love One Another." Does our continual militarization reflect our Creator's desire? If not, can we begin to create the livable environment He desires us to? Just think--transferring a large portion of our multibillion-dollar nuclear budget to quality mental health facilities would not only improve mental health, but would provide homes for a vast percentage of our homeless, along with reducing our illegal drug problem. Rather than imprison, we can heal those in need of our help. We are created to care, not to kill. Would this not be more humane and profitable for all? Using this approach to reduce our military budget, our children could all have quality schools with equitably paid teachers. Our bridges can be repaired. Hospitals could meet their societal needs. Our homeless could be cared for. This wonderful world is in our hands.

In 1995, our son's four-year battle with schizophrenia led him to the University of Washington Hospital, in Seattle. There, for the first time, Troy voluntarily requested treatment. After being confined in a tiny room for about two hours, while the medical staff formulated their refusal for intake plan, treatment was denied. Jerrie, his mom, was with Troy and requested involuntary treatment. Following two more hours, along with a mental evaluation, Troy was refused involuntary treatment. Seriously concerned about Troy's previous suicidal attempts, Jerrie told the mental health professional (MHP) "if you send him home Troy may take his life." This had no impact on the MHP's decision. The following day, Troy took his life. Twenty-five years later this situation has worsened on a larger scale. When will we, as a society care enough to reverse our lifestyles?

When will we, who vote leaders in power, become actively involved in reversing our national lifestyles from domination to inclusion?

Are nuclear weapons a compliment or a detriment to healthy lifestyles?

What hope do nuclear weapons provide for those suffering with mental illness, homelessness, hunger, cancer, aids, or the lack of an adequate income?

We, are their hope.

~

In God We Trust

The body of an eagle
Can only fly
When in unity
Both wings comply
To the concerns
Of the eagle's eye

For what the eagle sees
Determines its path
Favoring its needs
While avoiding wrath

Parental care
Perhaps the wisest on wings
Teaching their eaglets
Life's survival strings

Through life's durability
Eagles are wise
At middle age
They re-energize
Thus their longevity
Is no surprise

Continual surveillance
Of earth and sky
Their instinctive confidence
Is never shy

Their tenacious grip
Our founders grasped
As "In God We Trust"
We each are asked

With these grander qualities
Our founding fathers were wise
Challenging their citizenry
To reach for the skies

As on eagles' wings
Hope does soar
Sharing freedom
On every shore

Binding together
Humanity
On our eagles' wings
Of prosperity

As America's Eagles
Together we stand
Sharing and caring
For our motherland ~

~

Hand in Hand

Together we can
Bring peace to our land

But to do so
We must understand

Not all people
Share our plan

However it is not
Our plan

It is our Creator's plan
Even though
We don't understand

He asks us all
To walk
Hand in hand

This simple invitation
Can unite our land

By joining hands
Together we can ~

~

One Human Family

One nation, indivisible
Birthed before God
Willing to serve needs
At home and abroad

With pride in our stride
Some still hide
Tucked in the shadows
Of political or virtuous pride

As fresh breezes flow
Revealing the need,
Our time has come
To nurture new seed

With the fading
Of our once
Clouded nation
Comes in full view
Our multiple forms
Of discrimination

With the changing
Of the tide
Behind those clouds
We can no longer hide

Discrimination
Mingled with fear,
Gives rise to weapons
To many revere

Our housing of weapons
Fertilizes a two-way fear
Of oh so many
Some we hold dear

The arms God created
Are intended to hold
Never meant to fire
Or for profit be sold

So human arms
Are meant to extend
As we open doors
To welcome each friend

With this in mind
There is no need for war
Neither at home
Or on a foreign shore

Called as a world
To love one another,
The key to our survival
There is no other

As we recognize and erase
The need for fear and war
Caring and sharing
Can more easily
Slip through our door

Funds once spent on war
Now life do embrace
Producing healthy smiles
On many a face

Fully aware
Of varied paths
Our human survival
Requires less wrath

As God's gifts are shared
With earth's family
All life can live
As is meant to be

For if we believe
In God we trust
One human family
Is truly a must ~

~

The Breath of God

Wherever we travel
On Mother Earth
We witness life
In which God breathed birth

His spiritual hand
Picked up some land
Breathing into it
Gave life to man

From the male
Female was created
Through love's breath
Her lungs were inflated

Creativity unlimited
Life filled the ocean
Diversity walking
Countless wings in motion

Diversity
Designed by God
Why should individuals
View some as odd

Earth is a garden
Watered and nourished
Where our Creator desires
All life to flourish

Matters not
What color we bloom
Earth's bouquet
Has a pleasant perfume

Variety His plan
With hopes
We would understand
Life is the bouquet
Of our Creator's hand ~

~

Just Hoping,
Our Silence is Broken

Life's past
We cannot change
But human existence
Is in danger
If our future
We do not change

Our United Nations
Have sincerely spoken
Providing the pathway
For which many
Have been hoping

Our UN's silence is broken
The UN ratified a treaty
"The Treaty on the
Prohibition of Nuclear Weapons"
(TPNW)

This Treaty
Became effective
January 22, 2021

I know
Many excuses will flow
However
I'd like you to know
Government propaganda
Is as frigid as snow

Phrases like
"Strategic stability"
"Our deterrence"
"Second strike capability"
Are intentional camouflage
Intended to deceive
Hoping their lies
Many will believe

Do you really believe
Humankind will survive
A nuclear war
Healthy and alive

Our US bombs
Dropped on Japan
Set bodies on fire
Engraving a future
Not one of them
Did desire

While generating untold
Birth defects
Not to mention
Killing over
200,000 humans

Today's nukes
Are over 3,000 times
As powerful as those,
So, kiss your *** goodbye
Is the way it goes

Is this the life
We desire to live
Is this the will
To our children we give

Things won't change
Through our silent mode
Honesty revealed
The truth must be told

Nuclear weapons
Are life's most serious threat
More deadly deception
Is impossible to get

For our children's sake
Let our silence be broken
In doing so
Let the truth be spoken ~

~

Unity

It is time for our world
To put aside male dominance
As we walk together
With a common oneness

For our human bouquet
Cannot succeed
Unless togetherness
Is what we breed

So if humanity
Desires to thrive
Unconditional acceptance
Must be our bride

For in a marriage
As two become one
Living in unity
Is much more fun ~

~

The Silent Unthinkable

In our COVID-19 silence
accompanied by human indifference
a far more deadly threat sleeps.

It flies, floats, and sleeps in our soil.
Camouflaged as security
it is anything but.

Fences, cameras,
and armed guards secure
this secret threatening danger.

It's transported nationally
in camouflaged guarded semis,
on a web of highways,
hoping to remain invisible.

Nested near some population centers,
some tucked in the woods,
peppering America
as never they should.

Perhaps it is time,
before it's too late,
to ask ourselves
fully honest and straight,

Is our silence unthinkable
truly useable?

Are our nation's
6,800 nuclear weapons
for protection,
or self-annihilation

~

Reflection Fourteen
Our Priorities

There is a serious social and spiritual contradiction in our individual, local, national, and worldly approach to our survival. By criminalizing mental illness, we inflict far more harm on both the individual and the family. From our blame comes their shame, magnifying their pain.

As a society we demean and imprison family members while they simply need our compassion, understanding, and assistance. Our son Troy experienced unjustifiable imprisonment several times, simply for having a mental illness beyond his control. Do we send people to prison for having a heart atack or cancer? Are injured athletes transported from football fields to locked jail cells? Mental illness is also a serious medical condition, but we send many of these seriously ill patients to jail, or our unforgiving back alleys and cold, wet streets. Why? We have the resources to provide the medical care they need. Please, let us adjust our priorities and care for each other.

~

Oh, What a World

Together we can
Prepare and propose
A productive plan
To dismantle and remove
Nuclear weapons from our land

In doing so
Excess funds can flow
To human needs
Setting healed lives aglow

For it will be grand
When judges and protesters
Stand hand in hand,
Both respecting human worth
Across our mother land

And as we bury
Differences of heart
Human needs
Receive a fresh start

As the shredding of fences
Sharpens our senses
Once walled indifference
Can share park benches

No longer alone
With an illness of mind
We will restore a gentleness
We once left behind

Oh, what a world
Humanity can be
Blooming together
Quite happily ~

~

Living Bouquets

Life's bouquets
Become far more attractive
When varied shapes and colors
Become interactive

A song from here
A dance form there
Blended menus
Potluck variety to share

Oh the stories
From cultures galore
Blended clothes
We do adore

As fragrances flow
From the human bouquet
Refreshing memories
Float our way

I've been there
And so have you
Sharing bouquets
With many or few

Celebrations
Or time for sorrow
Memories to share
Today and tomorrow

Living bouquets
Brighten the day
As togetherness
Is what they display

Differences
Matter not
When unity
Is truly sought ~

~

Reflection Fifteen
E pluribus Unum

It is through giving that one will receive. It is up to us the path we pave, as goodbye to dominance we joyfully wave. From COVID's quite distancing, as we spend more time listening blooms a new norm, soft, quiet, gentle, and warm. No matter the political weather, we are in this together. As we compost indifference and rage, together let us open a fresh new page. In healing our divide, let us step forth in pride. E pluribus Unum (out of many one) is much more fun, as "In God We Trust" blooms forth, from His smiling Son.

~

Reflection Sixteen
Attitudinal Change
Can Happen

As a child raised in rural northern Wisconsin our dad drove our family to a Catholic church in South Superior, Wisconsin, every Sunday. Even when the snow was thick and sometimes drifting, we attended mass. My first and half of my second grade was in a one-room school where one teacher taught all six grades. It was wonderful! All the boys had a serious crush on our beautiful teacher who was fresh out of college and so sweet. In my second grade, when she became engaged, many little boys hearts were broken.

When not frozen, the well in front of the school provided our drinking water. We had one bucket and one ladle which everyone shared. When the weather began to freeze a neighbor filled the bucket from their sheltered well. The separate outhouses behind the school provided sex education. Behind the girl's bathroom the guys peaked through the knotholes in the single-layered wall.

In my second grade, following Christmas break, a new school opened, combining three rural one-room schools in a spacious new building containing all eight grades. We even had flush toilets, a drinking fountain, and hot lunches. My mom was one of the three cooks. The cooks wheeled a long table down the straight hall, serving lunches to one grade at a time. Eating a warm lunch in our classrooms was amazing. This is where individual differences first became visible to me. There were only two of us in a large classroom that said grace before eating. It wasn't long before I said grace so no one would notice, skipping the sign of the cross. I didn't like being teased.

As years progressed, I became aware that there were only four Catholic students noticeable to me in the entire school. One was my younger brother Milton. It appeared that the majority never went to church as there were few churches around. Internally, I was truly proud of my faith which had helped me through some rough times. Publicly, I apologetically avoided embarrassing behavior.

As an adult, looking in my rearview mirror, I relate my childhood to a form of discrimination. Attending all-white schools through the tenth grade I was unexposed to varied skin tones and ethnic differences. I could mask my religion, while races and cultures cannot hide their differences. So, my experience is limited. However, I wonder if, unlike my childhood behavior, individuals can surface their self-pride at early ages, life could be more welcoming. I am not proud of stuffing my inner pride as a child, because I know I allowed it to raise obstacles.

In my tenth through twelfth grade, I attended a Catholic high school. Here I became painfully aware that I lived on a farm and not in the "city." The "farm-boy" attitude was most prevalent in some staff, even if they were nuns. I could sense it from some students, but not the majority. Living in town neither the students or staff had an idea what it was like get a ride to town on your dad's way to work, arriving one and a half hours before school started, or too often hitchhike the twelve miles home after school. The public high school was one block away from the Catholic school, but I was not allowed ride on their public-school bus. Even though it stopped near my home to both pick up and drop off neighboring friends.

During basic military training I began to surface my pride by attending mass. It has taken years to totally address and change my childish attitude. Today, in my late seventies, I wish I had conquered this as a child.

While stationed in San Antonio, Texas, during basic training, discrimination became extremely visible. One of the young men is our barracks was continually harassed by a few. After several weeks of watching this, I spent some time with this individual. I discovered he was Jewish, which drew out the meanness of several others. It wasn't long before I saw them mess up his locker just moments prior to a barrack inspection. Following the inspection, I confronted those involved explaining that their actions had just resulted in our entire barracks receiving demerits. It was their behavior, not his, that resulted in our low score.

During basic training, another event boldly planted images in my mind. It was mid-summer in 1962. The temperature was daily over 100 degrees, thus no local residents were attending the baseball games, so we were invited to attend. This was a way to get off the Base for a few hours, so several of us volunteered. The local residents were right; it was way too hot to sit in the open-air bleachers, so we gathered in the shade under the bleachers. Wow, I still wish I had had a camera. The restrooms and fountains were individually labeled "White," "Black," and "Other." The custodian explained "the other applied to Mexicans." Living in the north I had never seen anything this divisive.

It would be a blessing to our world if childish ridicule and hurtful teasing would stop. It would truly be a blessing if all individuals could ignore painful ridicule and teasing at all ages. I know, this is easy for me to say as a Caucasian and not having fully experienced being discriminated against in multiple ways. However, we must recognize and discuss discrimination to be able to address and eliminate it.

Not all forms of discrimination apply directly to children, but they may have an indirect affect through adult or parental influence. The following is a list of many forms of discrimination:

Cultural	Social class
Economic	Education
Sexual	Marital
Ethnic origin	Employment
Racism	Wage
Gender	Physical appearance

Disability	Religion
Illness	Age
Ideological	And others

Perhaps this is a marginal way of viewing discrimination, but I have seen it to be quite effective. Having experienced over 20 years in Seattle schools' classrooms with behaviorally disadvantaged youth of varied ethnicities, I have watched the "bait and hook personalities" numerous times as fights broke out. On a larger scale, it is what Donald Trump was, and remains, quite proficient at. Trump is a seasoned fisherman when throwing out insults as bait. The media shares it as "breaking news", filling Trumps nets with fish. Chaos and confusion grows. If the bait could be ignored, the one fishing would foolishly retreat. Perhaps the line would be quickly tossed again, but there is no real need to bite this poisoned hook. I know quite well some individuals fish with weapons and the danger is extreme and perhaps deadly, but if ignoring the bait could be taught at early ages, more deadly incidents could be reduced.

Having visited a student in Seattle's Harborview Hospital who had just had a portion of his skull removed so his swollen brain could heal after having a bullet crease his skull, I am no stranger to violence. Had this young man ignored those in the car yelling at him, he may have been at home instead of in a guarded emergency unit.

The content of this book focuses on weapons. Discrimination is a weapon. Perhaps we need to address it as such and reduce its destructive power.

Attitudinal change needs to be taught at early ages and reinforced during the maturing process. The roots of discrimination are deep, but we can change if we start early. Change can become a blessing.

Conclusion

Wikipedia has an encompassing definition of discrimination worth copying and sharing.

Discrimination

"Discrimination is the act of making unjustified distinctions between human beings based on the groups, classes, or other categories to which they are perceived to belong. People may be discriminated on the basis of race, gender, age, or sexual orientation, as well as other categories. Discrimination especially occurs when individuals or groups are unfairly treated in a way which is worse than other people are treated, on the basis of their actual or perceived membership in certain groups or social categories. It involves restricting members of one group from opportunities or privileges that are available to members of another group."

~

In applying this definition to today's society, let us expand on a few forms of discrimination boldly occurring and reoccurring on a regular basis.

Native Americans, the original citizens of North America, were slaughtered and placed on reservations, for the sake of white European "progress." This painful process continues today as Native Americans are deprived of their inalienable rights.

Africans were captured, bought, sold, raped, and tortured for profitable desires. This abusive behavior continues as innocent individuals are denied human rights, shot in the back, knelt on, frequently arrested, and far more disgusting treatment, under the white supremacy desire to controal.

Sexual orientation is painful and unnecessary. We may be able to change our exterior jeans, but we cannot change our interior genes.

Individuals suffering with a mental illness are neglected and negatively labeled due to our deliberate lack of medical understanding and necessary medical treatment.

The unjust Chinese and Japanese treatment and internment.

U.S. abuse of neighbors seeking our help at our southern border.

Our needless deportation of immigrants and asylum seekers.

Our separation of children from their families.

Our camouflaged "might makes right" belief has been brainwashed into our nation's citizenry so weapons manufactures can reap profits at the expense of our innocent youth.

The cruel way we treat our Cuban neighbors is totally disgusting. These individuals and families have done nothing to deserve our abusive behavior.

Is this American pride something to be proud of or is it what we should apologize for, and correct? We, as Americans, do care and share. Can we make this our priority?

We, as individuals, as a society, as a nation, do accomplish so much we can truly be proud of. These kind deeds are just buds on plants seeking to bloom. Perhaps it is time to allow our true beauty to fully reveal itself. Our world looks up to the United States. Let us use this opportunity to bloom for our world as we produce an international garden.

**We are called
to love one another.**

**This is not exclusive
It is inclusive.**

~

Together We *Can*

Together
As fresh flowers we plant
Let us focus on *can*
In preference to can't

Individually and in unity we *can*,
Compost unsightly weeds
Replacing division
With fresh smiling seeds

Life is heaven's garden
Blooming, with colorful hope
Organic life
Which helps each other cope

As each of us
Plant hope as we may
Our individual gardens
Become one, inspirational bouquet

So together,
As fresh flowers we plant
Let us focus on *can,*
In preference to can't ~

The Roots of Our Nation

The soul of our nation
Has a slave planted foundation
These seeds of evil
Still sprout separation

This fact
We truly must own
But needless to say
No longer condone

As liberty's nest
In our tree of life
Longs to hatch equality
Free of strife

Where wings can soar
Free of storms
Guided by the spirits
Of multiple forms

Where birds do flock
With no one to mock
And division is unified
With compassionate talk

Where seeds from the tree
Of liberty
Can sprout and bloom
Hassle free

This truly can be
Our reality
Its potential depends
On each you and me

Fertilizing the roots
Of liberty ~